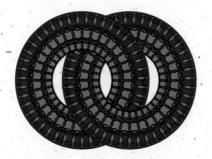

SEE THE WOLF

SEE THE WOLF

SARAH SOUSA

CavanKerry ❖ Press LTD.

CavanKerry Press Ltd.
Fort Lee, New Jersey
www.cavankerrypress.org

Publisher's Cataloging-In-Publication Data
(Prepared by The Donohue Group, Inc.)
Names: Sousa, Sarah.
Title: See the wolf / Sarah Sousa.
Description: First edition. | Fort Lee, New Jersey : CavanKerry Press Ltd., 2018.
Identifiers: ISBN 9781933880662
Subjects: LCSH: Sousa, Sarah—Poetry. | Mothers and daughters—Poetry. | Single mothers—Poetry. | Women—Abuse of—Poetry. | Nineteen eighties—Poetry. | Fairy tales—Poetry.
Classification: LCC PS3619.O878 S44 2018 | DDC 811/.6—dc23

Cover artwork by Meredith Sibley
Cover and interior text design by Ryan Scheife, Mayfly Design
First Edition 2018, Printed in the United States of America

CavanKerry Press is dedicated to springboarding the careers of previously unpublished, early, and mid-career poets by bringing to print two to three Emerging Voices annually. Manuscripts are selected from open submission; CavanKerry Press does not conduct competitions.

CavanKerry Press is grateful for the support it receives from the New Jersey State Council on the Arts.

ALSO BY SARAH SOUSA

Church of Needles (2014)
The Diary of Esther Small, 1886 (2014)
Split the Crow (2015)

For Mom and Jess, for the three of us

If you join two lives, there is oft a scar,
They are one and one, with a shadowy third
—ROBERT BROWNING

CONTENTS

III SHE KNOWS PERFECTLY WELL HOW TO RUN

SEE THE WOLF

I

LIKE A DOCENT

OF THE BODY

SELF PORTRAIT WITH MABEL, ROSE, LILLIANNE, FERN, MILDRED, BEA

My mother named me
little old lady. Named me
startle-easily, little-flincher,
night-terrors-with-spiders.
I lived in a different century.
I was born rural
in a city of mills.
My mother named me
place of unreachable hills.
A temperance movement of one,
I was sober
as spring water. I was old
then I was older.
My mother named me
may-your-body-never-
surprise-you-with-want.
I was her easy pregnancy, asleep
by eight, awake when convenient.
I held the fetal position
like a moral obligation:
her ribs were unmolested
as a Victorian birdcage. They pried
my soft bones like ancient pottery
from between my mother's hips
while she slept. An orphaned monkey,
a baby of the '70s,
I sucked the bright orange nipple
of a sterilized glass bottle, held
by some other woman
while my mother came-to. She named me
Mabel, Rose, Lillianne, Fern, Mildred, Bea—
names I wear like tarnished jewelry
pinned to the inside
of my bra for safekeeping.
They take turns speaking

through my mouth, choose
my handbags, prefer flat shoes.
They embody the word *habit*,
placing a napkin atop my glass
of water, one beneath to absorb the sweat,
carry a magnifying glass
to read menus. With them
I'm always the youngest in the room.
And nothing changes. They name me not-yet-
born, but predict a natural birth.
They ask:
do you believe us?
does it help you to believe in us?

OPAL

We were in the yellow car, palest yellow
like lemon meringue pie, shiny yellow-shelled candy
jawbreaker. You said the car was called an *Opal*.
Dad parked it on the steep hill near the cellar door:
wait here I'll be right back. The cellar door,
low like the door to a cave or tomb,
dad had to duck his head to disappear. Cinder block cool,
the cellar had a fragrant antique dust like books.
You waited with me. The car's front end pointed uphill,
so we were tipped back in our seats, off-kilter,
roller-coaster style. Would the emergency brake hold?
And that car (mid-1970s?)
did it even have an emergency brake? No
seatbelts. I felt the stillness give, an inch,
slow slide against resistance. I knew
when the car started to roll, gain speed
backwards, gravity would have me
pinned at the center, where the soul
and future ghost reside, to my vinyl seat—
my arms and legs thrown forward like a cartoon
character catching a cannon ball.
And I guess you couldn't stop it.
Or you weren't sitting up front.
I guess I was alone.
At the bottom of the hill there was a lake.

TOM AND JERRY

I think it's safe to disclose our secret word
ruined now that it's popular slang for the drug MDMA.
We thought we were tricky making our word a phrase,
the one the neighbor gave if Mom couldn't pick me up
from Pop Warner cheerleading practice.
Our mother of the escape plan from movie theaters
and malls had no special instructions if she just plain forgot
to pick me up and I sat in the deepening dusk
beside the junior high ripping handfuls of grass out
at the roots to make a nest, or collecting pencils
kids had dropped from the windows. The implied course
of action when forgotten seemed to be the same as when lost:
don't panic, don't talk to strangers, don't accept candy
or rides from strangers (unless you want to end up
on a milk carton), stay where I last saw you,
beside the junior high—which, I guess she didn't know,
lacked a special force field against predation—
reading folded notes kids had thrown from the windows:
bite me, help, kill me now.
I might have enjoyed the quiet, the purpling
sky if I wasn't so timid, seen some humor
in the scenario that had me terrified: a dark car pulls up,
a man opens the door, says the words
that mean *you're mine.*

MEAT MARKET

It's one of those nights your mother and her friend preen,
too close to the mirror—sparkly silver tops, tight jeans.
And the eye shadow's heavy, the heels high.
Hair picks mid-tease one of them says *meat market*,
they laugh. They leave, and the daughters ages ten to fourteen
turn up the radio, turn on the TV; each alone
in her own fantasy. Your mother and her friend work part time
at an exercise studio in a strip mall. One full wall is a mirror,
another a window where men coming from the liquor store look in.
All the instructors wear black leotards and tights, lead ladies
in high kicks, bends, sit ups, full straddles; chant the mantra
we must, we must, we must increase our busts. The only exercise
machine is one you stand on like a scale, a wide canvas belt
around your waist vibrates fat away. The six women
who work here eat only canned green beans. They're dieting.
At ten, your arm is bigger than Leah's thigh. You learn
the word *anorexic*. The women are single, divorced or separated, all
on the market. The studio's logo is the caricature of a woman
in leotard: tiny body bulging in the right places, big hair.
It's one of those days you learn too much just by listening
to women talk, chant the mantra for the first time, get laughed at.

THE ME GENERATION

70s and 80s T-shirt slogans

Do it in the dirt
Frankie says relax
I like champagne, Cadillacs, cash
Bowlers do it in the alley
Love a nurse today
Flash a friend today
Young and tender
Bored to death
Joggers do it on the run
I gave my body to science but they gave it back
Itty bitty titty club
Why can't I be rich instead of good looking?
7th-graders do it better
Band members like to play all day
Barely wet
Falling drunk
Do it with a pig
Always a lady
Like a virgin—yeah right!
Up your average
Orgasm donor
Cute and cuddly
Operation turn on
Freshmen do it better
Hairdressers say there are 69 ways to cut it
Die young stay pretty
Hug me I'm lonely
I know I'm efficient, tell me I'm beautiful
I may turn red but don't stop
I'm 21 buy me a drink
It's ok, I'm with the band
I'm fantastic in dark places
I'm giving up bowling for sex
I'm huggable
I'm ok God doesn't make junk

I'm the best available
I'm so horny even the crack of dawn looks good
Let's do it again
Juniors do it better
Once a king always a king but once a knight is enough
Sex instructor, first lesson free
Sex is like snow you never know how many inches you'll get or how long
it will last
Soccer players do it with more kicks
Sophomores do it better
Pussy wagon
Cocaine
Me
Smile if you had it last night
I may not go down in history but I'll go down on your little sister
Stay classy

POEM WITHOUT A FOREST

A man
in the dark
space
between
cement wall
and stunted pines—
filthy and gripping
the neck
of an empty bottle
of wine.
Scrubby growth
in a bed of red
mulch.
We watched him
watch us
through the rusted
branches
as we passed.
No one told
us not to,
but girls
know the first thing
about survival:
we only sometimes took that path.

PAW

His brothers called him Pete, after Peter Rabbit,
a kind of joke that stuck.
Sundays, my mother, grandmother and I
ate sweets, sipped tea; all of us careful not to laugh
too loud or let our voices rise
because the house was just a four-room cottage
and Paw slept late.
From Oklahoma, he had a drawl. *Paw paw*
was a Southern endearment he taught me to call him;
it never felt natural. In photos,
his ancestors stood barefooted in red dust
outside slapped-together shacks.
My mother said he'd had a hard childhood,
his parents didn't even name him.
Around noon, Paw would emerge
from his bed, squinty-eyed, wiry gray hair
standing on end. He was long and lean
and sometimes mean. He scared me.
Sundays, he grunted in reply
to my grandmother, sliced through her
cheerfulness with one cruel comment
then disappeared into the basement
where he pursued his hobbies. Or he'd linger,
pacing between the small front rooms,
coming near our table. Sometimes he'd want to hug me
and I would rise reluctantly,
let him pull me against his sinewy body.
His smell was sharp and made my heart knock.
My mother looked uneasy but laughed
and chattered for my grandmother's sake.
I couldn't read her.
If Paw hugged me right in front of them, was that ok?
We looked like someone who stays
when she knows perfectly well how to run.

THE GIRL LATER KNOWN AS RED

The way she was digested
like any other meat
didn't make it into Disney.
Hungry, dirty, already missing teeth,
she would not have grown into
our heroine even if she hadn't been killed
and eaten in 1590 by a man
suffering from lycanthropy.
A man who *believes* he's a wolf
must be hanged then sliced open
to see if he wears his pelt on the inside.

They never found the girl whole,
curled up sleeping like a bean.
And she surely didn't escape
by her own wits. The original: a crude
cautionary tale based on recent,
gruesome murders; like girls
on milk cartons, pretty hitchhikers
later found in some guy's basement,
razor blades in candy apples.

A SPLIT

We met her in the parking lot
of a store we never shopped at.
She carried it like a water balloon
wrapped in a thin receiving blanket,
fresh from the hospital.
First my father held
the baby, next he softly cried,
but tried to hide it. Then
I know you've always wanted a brother
like
your mother and I need to live apart. A split-
level fits two single mothers,
a clutch of daughters,
one Doberman
chained to the first-floor railing.

OUR LADY OF PINE SOL AND BLEACH

Time capsule of the broken family,
dollhouse of the newly divorced—
a just-closed-on-condo with wall to wall
carpet, used beta player,
papasan chair like an adult-sized cradle.
In order and cleanliness we achieve control,
so the condo also contains obsessive exercise
regimes, 500-calorie-diets, one powerful
vacuum used daily, throw pillows,
and all things whose scent says *clean*:
candles, potpourri, deodorizers, Pine Sol, bleach.
Some days you might detect an odor of pressure-
cooked meat and cabbage, or cat box.
But we have more bleach and mom says
let the potpourri boil 'til the pan burns dry;
scrape the black petals out with a knife.
My father is gone
and I feel unsafe. But my mother
just got back from the gym.
She's down on her knees cleaning.

GIRLS' SIDE

Round face framed by the short cut
that made kids tease she was the new boy
at school; the dodge-ball court's gravel
embedded, purple in both palms,
red welt slammed onto her fat thigh—mark
of the lazy in the path of the ball's certain
trajectory; can't move their asses fast enough.
Later she would keep gray doves, overlong,
'til their shy cooing became full throttled
weeping or raw-throated hunger. A tenement
mews graffitied with bird-lime, absent the magic
of homing. To avoid the fanfare
required on their circling return, she never
released them. Always the fat girl inside,
concerned with her own comfort, always
that shameful hunger.
And the ones she would choose
to play the game with
are the ones who couldn't
bear to go on
whipping the ball at each other's heads.
It's fast and supposed to be fun.
Stop whimpering.
No one was ever in danger.
No one's injuries were ever so bad
that she died
on the girls' side of the playground.

HONEY DIPPED

Grandma and Paw had an octagonal
coffee table with drawers on every side
and cabinet doors that led into one
undivided space, large enough for us to hide in.
The glass top was beveled and caught
the light like cubic zirconia.
Besides the honey dipped donuts,
and Grandma telling us to eat
as much as we wanted, the octagonal
table was the best part of our visits.
We sat barelegged on the thick orange carpet. I don't want to
scare you, or mess with your memories, but the fact is
the carpet was the color of dried blood.
That carpet muffled every noise.
All the books in the cabinet were oversized picture books,
the classics: Hansel and Gretel, Cinderella, Snow White,
Little Red Riding Hood, Sleeping Beauty.
Gigantic books, about our height. I think it was a trend
at the time. The characters, overblown and distorted,
heads two-feet tall, leered out from the pages.
And not just the princes and villains, even Happy
and Bashful, the candlesticks, teapot and cushions;
Grandma before the wolf even.

SISTERS, 1980s

Sometimes they're Cabbage Patch plastic,
sometimes figurine porcelain, Shirley Temples and cherry
nail polish on New Year's Eve. Always awake
when the ball drops. Sometimes there's three,
sometimes two when the mother one decides
to be mother, clean house, dust and wash the floors
on hands and knees, the rag and dragged pail behind her.
When she lights the potpourri burner
they know what that means. Alone,
the sisters eat all the groceries, the carbs
they call *starches*, grow into their swear words;
one fat and quiet, the little one mouthy.
They develop their neuroses with help
from the mother's boyfriend, the smug vice
principal who's drawing the line
between them and *college material*,
the father, his girlfriend: always his girlfriend.
Not late to the game, she created the game.
Sometimes they're Cyndi Lauper,
sometimes Cindy Crawford, the glittery stickers
in the sticker collection, the scented:
Aqua Net, Aussie, Baby Soft.
They've been watching *Three's Company*
since they were seven, *General Hospital* since eight
and though one is four years older,
in the apartment alone after school,
they're the same age. They know
what it means when creepy Mr. Roper makes eyes
at Jack and poses his hands like birds.
They know that Luke was Laura's rapist. Everyone does.
Woman-raised and like certain dogs, they don't trust men.
They carry the key for the bolt lock.
They let themselves in.

II

THEY MAKE

BEAUTIFUL SCARS

Thus life is spent . . .
In being touch'd, and crying—Don't!

—WILLIAM COWPER

YOU ARE NOT GRASS

The last wild passenger pigeon was named
Buttons because the mother of the boy who shot it,
stuffed the bird and sewed black buttons for eyes.

People with Ekbom syndrome imagine
they're infested with mites.

It's possible the entire Buttons family
developed Ekbom, an aspect of which is
folie à *deux* (madness between two),
where a person in contact with the sufferer
develops symptoms—as in an *actual* infestation.

All wild things have kleptophobia:
the fear of being stolen, as well as cleithrophobia:
the fear of being trapped. I did, after
the divorce and my mother began dating—
fear of being adopted by a man
wearing *slacks* and old fashioned shoes, (automaton
ophobia?) who winked at me and promised to return
my mother at a decent hour. Whose accent
was Southern, who pronounced his R's
so long they became words in their own right,
words at the ends of words; his R's
like grappling hooks, like a crocodile-
purse with yellow eyes.

Why is the fear of being trapped a clinical phobia,
while the compulsion to slit
and stuff a thing not listed in the DSM?

Nature permanence is the healthy acceptance
that you are not grass but human, beneficial
if you suffer from hylophobia (fear of trees)
not so helpful if you have Cotard delusion
and know you're not only human, but a corpse.
Related to Cotard is xenomelia: the feeling
that one's limbs don't belong to the body,
chirophobia: fear of hands. And worse,

apotemnophilia, where a person disowns
the limbs, yearns to live life

as an amputee. Why the insistence
that an animal have black buttons,
yellow marbles, key holes for eyes?
that its entrails be replaced with horsehair
and rags? that the peppery dots
swarming the blanket aren't mites? What are the chances
that a man who flashes his teeth when he talks
doesn't bite? To fear is animal.

To create out of fear must be human—
slits to let the mites out,
steel shot like beautiful beadwork
studding lavender breasts. Phantom limbs
when real hands become too dangerous.

RED

smear in the wolf's throat.

In one version she's found in the *company* of wolves,
not in their stomachs, bedraggled but dozing
like the offspring of wolves
on the wiry back of an alpha.

In the traditional version, after flirting
with danger, after giving up
grandmother's coordinates,
knowing the wolf will await her,
after the seduction, the devouring,
she chooses survival. Or maybe
she chooses both, wants first to feel herself
held in the wolf's throat.

Which version has her punching holes
in the wolf's stomach with a pencil,
snatched from the bedside table
when she knew the ruse was up
and scribbled a note for help,
as if writing the fragment of a dream
for later? In my version,

I'll include how it feels to be eaten,
the entering isn't clean—
teeth are like dull keys.
The wolf opens you
            to your own red
glister like a docent of the body.

BECAUSE FEMALE BLOOD IS FUNNY

During the fast drive to the emergency room
my wound bled freely onto the cloth car seat,
the stain spread, stiffened as it dried. Days later,
slipping into the passenger's side,
my mother's male friend laughed, said:
looks like someone had her period.

LIKE A NAME

I can say I didn't look because I didn't want to
see my own blood. But now that I think about it,
I did look, once I was safe on the white gurney—
tight sheets, smell of bleach; the doctor's cool
gloved fingers touching jagged skin around the edges
of the wound. I kept calling her *Mrs.* instead of *Doctor*
because the only doctor I'd ever known was the white-haired
male pediatrician I'd had since birth
who told my mother at every checkup
that I should lose some weight, then winked at me
and stuck a lollipop behind my ear. He'd just consulted
with my Mrs. doctor, swept aside the curtain
and declared they would *operate.*
My mother heard *amputate.* IV in,

I counted down; between seven and six remembered
a spring day at the playground beside the river: my mother,
my sister, me, and an Asian man sitting on a park bench
who talked to us in broken English.
He pointed at my skinny, dark haired sister and all but said, *meh.*
But when he looked at me he beamed; his generous gestures
made of me some kind of child Botticelli.
He sat beside us, happy to pat my hand, my knee,
as though I was his own well-fed child. My mother grew uneasy,
packed up our picnic and rushed us away. I got to five
when the liquid crossed my eyes, I may have died. I heard someone say
the dog bit me instead of my sister because I had more meat.
Someone said the dog would have taken her whole leg.
I felt a proper sacrifice, woke with wet gauze swathing my tongue.
Stitches like whiskers poked from the bandage;
infection sewn in like a name on a sleeve.

TO THE COMEDIAN WHO CALLED THELMA
AND LOUISE TWO WHITE HEIFERS

My mother dreamed of wrenching jaws open with her small hands.
I could see it gave her some pleasure. A pleasure
all women share imagining their strength in the face of danger.
My moments as prey were too recent,
I didn't wear the dog's hide beneath my clothes
for power. Though he had been *put to sleep,*
no one offered it to me. I wore an ugly scar
from seventeen stitches, a tender pink
entry wound newly sealed, a mark
that said *good eating.* I startled every time I heard
a keychain jingle: *dog loose.* I'd climb my mother like a tree.
If the dog materialized, worse, if it advanced, growling,
my mother would stand in front of me, arms splayed,
as if she were guarding someone
in a basketball game. But she wasn't fucking around.
My mother had practiced the maneuvers in her sleep,
the way she'd grasp the upper jaw with her right hand,
the lower with her left, and leverage her weight
at the hinges to crack the skull wide like a bivalve shell.
Don't laugh. Women have driven off cliffs,
burned men in their beds, to escape.
Her body over my body, my mother and the dog would face off.
I could feel the answering growl start deep inside her,
erupting in a voice not my mother's,
a voice to make us larger than we were. *Stronger*
than a scream, she'd said. A man laughed at us once.
But it wasn't him the dog obeyed.

THE FLAME

We hid at the neighbor's apartment, one over;
the woman who introduced me to the five-hundred-
calorie-a-day diet when I was thirteen,
teaching me the lifetime skill of micro managing
what I put in my mouth.

. . . because he smashed the Visions
Cookware he gave us for Christmas, set of smoke-
glass pans that afforded a window
onto the food's transformation as it cooked.
They were supposed to be shatterproof. The box said,
and plainly illustrated, that even the heat of a flame
under a pan of ice wouldn't cause a crack;
as though the ice, the pan, or flame itself understood self-restraint.
But he smashed them then cut himself with the pieces
in the upstairs bathroom. Blood on the vanity
our mother kept so clean.

At three o'clock *General Hospital*, at four *Phil Donohue*.
By the time the evening news came on at five,
we figured it was safe. Mom cleaned
the blood and glass, but not before we three crammed in the doorway
to see what we were dealing with, and make a plan
to spend less time at home: one week at Dad's,
two with friends in another state.
Did we think he'd never return,
that we'd baffle him with our absence?
We stoked the flame.

DON'T YOU FORGET ABOUT ME

I was fourteen that hot July night at the drive-in, watching *The Breakfast Club*;

you and my mother entwined up front. You were fun, you were young, you

would become obsessed and want to kill us, but this was before all that:

three of us eating popcorn in the unlit car. If I had to choose,

I'd say you were the line *don't you forget about me* in the Simple Minds song

while I took *will you stand above me* and worked it into nightmares:

a dark figure in an idling car, a dark figure at the door, in the house.

I was murdered in myriad ways: suffocation, fire, gunshot to the head. Maybe

you didn't realize that a daughter is housed inside her mother

like the smallest matryoshka doll, the pea-sized one; the way she looks out

from the same eyes, how a threat to one is a threat to the other.

But you were young, closer to my age than my mother's. And you were fun

when you weren't harming us. I kept the memory of that night long

past its usefulness: summer's short heat and the three of us singing

don't don't don't don't.

AN EMERGENCY IS HAPPENING

He burned it. What did he burn?
Our car. I think it's our car.
The apartment's alarm is so loud it splits
its own skull; air-raid loud. This is an *emergency.*
I am *unsafe.* He burned something. I think
he burned the car. The neighbors are coming out
wearing thin pajamas into the cool night,
the smoky air. They're alarmed.
Something's burning. Something
is on fire. Is our apartment on fire?
The walls are cinder block, fire-proof.
But something is on fire. A steeple
of flame reaches up into the trees,
singeing the leaves, singing
that oxygen-gorged, high-pressure hymn, and *pop*
the windows go. It's our car. The vinyl
dashboard and the plastic parts
are melting, the binder for History
I left on the back seat.
What about the gas tank?
We all step further back. I am barefoot
in the street. I am unsafe. But the car
is wholly brilliant with flame, irretrievably
on fire. My mother doesn't scream
or cry, when she moves her mouth it says, *my car is on fire.*
This is so stupid, my sister says.
In the distance sirens homing in.
Here they come, someone shouts. It's a party
fueled with gasoline, adrenaline.
The tires are melting.
Inside me someone wound
one of those matchbox cars beyond tight, cranked
back past the click that means it's broke,
a piece of junk, won't go.
But it goes.
Wheels and engine, wheels
and burning engine.
It goes.

CODEINE METEMPSYCHOSIS

Doubled in the bed, I couldn't fathom my extremis.
I turned to glass, took care not to thrash too much, thrashed,
picked shards of me out of the mattress.
Something pierced my thigh, a stitch, sharp
ceiling of smoke glass descended, collapsed.
I can't breathe. Someone lurked in the corner. *Is that me?*
I called. I was of two skins. Something climbed into the bed
beside me. In fever, I went so far inside
myself I slipped the barrier of me. I split in fourths,
eighths, sixteenths. Shaved thin as a finch
which flies straight into the glass.
I see the reflection of my finch determination, beak-
driven, coming at my face. Over and over my small
body dropped to the frozen ground, froze fast, my miraculous
feathers no more than winter waste: leaf matter, seed head, grass.
I formed a thin trickle, a diurnal stream of me:
here, here, here, here, and here. I queued up,
touched down in each of me. Yes, yes, yes, that's me.
Has your dog had its rabies shot? No
response, so I kept calling
into the void: *your dog just ate a piece of me,*
does he have rabies? Nothing.
He won't come back will he? Mom
I'm scared he'll come back,
can we get bolt locks and a chain, bullet-proof glass?
Mom, mom, mom, mom . . . *oh*
mom you've eaten the poisoned crumbs
not intended for you. Wake up. I'm having my worst nightmare.
I could follow the thin trail of you home,
but he knows where we live.

RUIN

A friend of the family my age hangs himself
in the woods behind his house,
leaves a note blaming his ex-girlfriend.
His mother finds him, destroys
the note, says, *I can't ruin that girl's life.*
Mothers lives are made for ruin.

THE HAIR BOYS SANG

So we joined a church, *open and affirming*, the kind
that ministered to gays, single women who wanted
to date and still be allowed to eat the body
of Christ every Sunday, and angry children
of broken families—at seven my sister
put on her bitch face, maintained it,
learned to apply makeup over it. In Sunday school,
sixth grade, you memorize the books of the Bible:
Genesis, Exodus, Leviticus, Numbers, Deuteronomy . . .
as far as I got without looking at Kirk Flint's lap
under the table, the Book open and hidden there.
His mother smoked a pipe. Twenty years later
he sat in a closed garage with a lawnmower running.
Kirk Flint who grabbed my ass in junior high,
as a joke, but who otherwise never taunted me.
I went to Kirk's funeral; open casket. He was dead,
but I'd say he looked awful before that: stringy hair
over a doughy face, everywhere else lumpy. I knew because
there were pictures on a poster board at the entrance,
only one as I remembered him: skinny kid with big sneakers.
All the boys at the time looked like drummers
in an 80s hair band. We sang a lot in Sunday school
and all the songs had pantomimes. *Make a joyful noise
unto the Lord, all the earth,* involved marching in place
and stomping as if we wanted to wake Christ
from his cave. *He arose a victor from the dark domain*
began with all of us crouching like animals
down near the cheap carpet, elbow to elbow
in a tight huddle, smirking probably then springing
as we commanded: *up from the grave he rise.*
He never even knocked twice for no, Kirk said
with a shake of his Van Halen hair.

SEE THE WOLF

He opened his jaws all sprent with blood . . .
He munch'd her heart he qauff'd her gore
and up her light and liver tore!

              —TALES OF TERROR, 1801

I

They would have my blood
be more than shocking, more
than drained. My pulse like harsh words softened.
Last I heard, my blood glowed, moon-limned,
though the moon was a sliver
rimed with ice. All agree, some substance
twisted in silvery ropes from the hole.
That phantasm soul?
but why (I
ask and have been asking since)
am I still here?

II

Good daughter, good on-the-verge-
of-wife (I *was* good. I didn't
see the wolf that night) tie my torn
apron tight. Up before the sun and I have out
all the spoons from their nesting,
drawer of broken bells thrown
wide. Sorry so abrupt, sorry for the clang
and racket. I startle like a teapot,
terrified hen, upset the living
with my molecular whirlwind.
My life's small detonation
permanently deafened (me?)
When you pray and weep I strain.
Pray and weep so I can translate
human whine to after-language.
Take some comfort in the insignificance
of your needs. Lined up by size,

these bent spoons make perfect mirrors:
the kitchen center-ward collapsing,
your astonishment turned upside down.

REAL FAIRY TALE

No one called me beauty before I was paired with the beast. I'm not beautiful. This isn't modesty. Once I was plucked from amongst the Beauty hopefuls, taken from home and seated at the head of a grand table beside the Beast, they groomed me, my virginal innocence became the tease, what audiences tuned-in to see. Some clucked and feigned worry for my safety, others thought the pairing *cute*, all salivated in anticipation, *will that be filmed too?* The juxtaposition of hunch-backed, bristling hyena/lion/man(?) with the mousiness of me, made for some great TV. They filmed us at table, they filmed us asleep, talking late into the night, riding horseback awkwardly. They filmed my visit home. I had forgiven my father and sisters for tricking me into the audition, declaring me a minor and stealing my paychecks. I thought once I got home I'd want to stay. But everything, though the same, was changed: the furniture duller, the rooms smaller. My sisters tried to bait me into telling the Beast's secrets, and when I wouldn't, into petty arguments; all so superficial and boring. No beauty lived in that place. I went back to the Beast. The film crew was hyped-up, working overtime in preparation for the big wedding episode. The long table in the ballroom, their ground zero, was littered from morning 'til night with platters and plates, half-eaten food, chicken bones, stuffed ashtrays, crusts, crumbs, and empty cans of Red Bull; the crew, like swine at the trough. I tried to stay out of the way. Where once I dreaded the season finale, now I was all nervous anticipation, like a real bride eager for her wedding night. I felt tenderer and tenderer toward my beast, letting my hand stray to his muscular thigh beneath the table, laughing more; even the feel of the wiry hair that stood up on his thick neck, which once repulsed, now stippled me with electricity, through my arm, down one side of my body. The wedding couldn't come soon enough. That night, the church fairly sparked for me, flooded with light, cameras positioned to capture every conceivable angle. The Beast grunted, fumbled the ring onto my finger. I beamed, said *I do . . .* and then, as if this were a 7th birthday party with everyone shouting *surprise,* instead of my wedding, the beast shrank before my eyes. I stumbled back, shook my head, tried to take in air. The cameras were rolling. But I couldn't squint away the small pink man standing in beast's overlarge suit, hair smooth, features finely cut and handsome. He reached a hand out, I recoiled. He said, *Beauty, don't you recognize me?* I did see the Beast lurking in his eyes. *I just need a little time,* I said, trembling. *I'll have to get used to this.* Everyone laughed. I took his soft hand in mine. I couldn't help whispering for only the two of us to hear: *what have you done with Beast?* As if the whole thing were a practical joke this stranger might let me in on. *Where is my* real *other half?* I wanted to yell in his pretty face. *I'm no meat for your mowing.* The prince just laughed, exposing his straight white teeth. The cameras loved him. As the priest finished the ceremony and the cameras followed us back down the aisle the way we had come, hoping to catch a besotted expression (I hated to disappoint them), I tried to focus on the ardent prince's eyes and couldn't shake the feeling that the Beast was trapped inside. I was ready to pry open his skull with a crow bar and set my beast free. Even the film crew fist-pumped, threw confetti. I became convinced they were all in on it. The writers intended this to be Season One's finale. If some other virgin had gotten the part, she'd have been just as duped, just as beautiful. It was written in the script, as was my coupling with *Ardent.* His last gig must have been a toothpaste commercial, or pushing some kind of drug for enhancement, why else that smile rending his face. The cameras would have us in the Beast's bed, Episode One, surrounded by candelabra. Me: still virginal, still mousy. Then the fun would start. The producers wanted to carry this thing through a second season on Ardent's prowess, and they wanted me to play along. Close-up on my transformation from virgin to whore. They probably intended to end the last episode with me back in that bed, legs splayed, some human baby dragging my darkness out for all to see. Flashback, close-up on my transformation from maiden to mother: setting it right. But I could still feel Beast's tough hide beneath my hand. And what I want to know is this: where does the banished self reside when change is wrought? To get through even the first episode of Season Two, I knew I would have to go there. Find my Beast.

III

SHE KNOWS
PERFECTLY WELL
HOW TO RUN

THE WRECK

The women had no choice
but to fashion a family, name strewn rock
a trail they could follow
home. They dressed each other's wounds,
sewed cormorant feathers into garments with needles
of bone. Each carried a two-note whistle
from the keeled sternum of a gull.

The initial survivors numbered in the hundreds:
prisoners and their soft-fingered keepers,
clerks, botanists, orphans; the violent and the meek.
A microcosm of society foundered on the rocks;
the jagged south spit skewering their vessel.

Let's reckon the rescue in decades.
The ship, when it reached them, no more
than batten boards taunting the sea, weather
congealing into dark eyes above and beneath.
By that time, there were seven women
and one baby, not yet weaned. A bright day
on the Pacific, 18th century. Legend says
the men diminished rapidly to five
and then to one, after a makeshift escape
boat capsized just outside the bay. Whereupon
the lone man declared himself king
and set about raping every woman in turn.

No one recalls the names of the women,
the babies born and buried.
The final seven we know only as a slim majority:
a steel blade and six knives made of shell.

METAMORPHOSIS

I wrote the book *On Sex*
published under my husband's name,
of course. I invented *the* technique
for weaving silk, fashioned a dress
like the finest spider's web to cover a woman
but reveal her completely. *The all-
lover, rapacious,* some whispered; as if
I could be defined—
shamefuller and shamefuller, by my appetites.
In modern times, I'd be *that* woman
wearing the parchment-
thin T-shirt: *man eater;* and braless.

Solanum, aconite, somniferum,
belladonna, opium, the baby fat of girls:
          a salve
for skin, when skin
isn't wanted. A salve for encouraging
          pin feathers.
When a man rubs it on, he turns into an ass,
hide-bound, ridden by fleas. On my skin
it glimmers, it glimmers
in my hair, causes convulsions.
My arms lift without consent, spread
to test their span, great muscles form
at the hinges. A burning, an undulation wracks my body;
sharp quills pierce from the inside out,
blossom into intricate bracts and branches,
the downy bloom of breath feathers gently blown.
My nose hardens into sharp beak, pink nails to talons.
Permeable skin, which relies on the touch
of another for electricity, can't rival my 8,000 feathers,
45,000 nerve endings aroused by the wind.
No mortal woman has felt the pure, lambent
burn-through of mounting the wind.
Else, there would be no mortal women.

MORE THAN THE WEIGHT OF
ITS LADEN BRANCHES

The cottage has an apple tree and textbooks
in the attic, a couch slashed by bars of sun
where I lie tragic as a wine spill.
Because I fear discovery by the man
who mows the lawn, I keep my routine
simple: wake early with the birds,
wash in the stream, harvest water and apples.
Keep out of sight, conserve energy.
Three apples a day times twenty years equals . . .
When I stand too quickly the room goes
dim. In autumn I pick the tree
clean, store the apples in a pillowcase
for winter. I move like a ghost
behind faded curtains, ration my reading,
ration the apples, and make lists
in a black address book: embolism, sharp
cheddar, rhizome, cell division, linguini and clams.
I write: I know I will die of starvation
and should leave here. I stay.
I write: God is sending a husband
and wishes me to wait for Christmas.
Three apples a day times three months
equals . . . I wait. Christmas comes,
the new year, clumps of hair in the bed.
I believe the remedy to be profuse
sunshine and love. I believe I will
die of starvation. Twenty days ago
I ate the last apple. It's cold
but the chickadees will sing me
(nobody-nobody-nobody) through winter.
I stop reading. I follow, on hands and knees,
the sun as it moves through the rooms,
lie down in its patches. The heater's breath
grows shallower every day.
I know I should leave but don't.
For one: I can no longer stand,

two: it's so peaceful here. I have everything
I ever wanted—an apple tree equals
more than the weight of its laden branches.
When my husband arrives we'll add
a garden and a smokehouse. My heart-
beat slows to an icicle's thin drip. I write:
whoever finds my body should know
this was a case of domestic violence.

CATS KILL BIRDS FOR ME

In this house
when someone says she, he means me.
I'm the only she in a houseful of he(s)
When is she making dinner? or *She's in the bath*
(the garden, the car), she wants to be alone.
If I'm within earshot,
I give myself away. Cats kill birds,
it's what they do, but I think my cats
kill birds for me. They know I collect feathers
into feather bouquets. They know I like a fan
of wings. I don't like gore,
so they won't leave that on the doorstep;
sometimes the feathers are still attached
to some skin. When I'm in the kitchen,
(she's making dinner) sounds of cooking:
I give myself away. Cats kill,
I know. I especially like the under-feathers
birds don't display and don't drop with ease:
the pure white feathers at a chickadee's throat,
the tiny yellow-tipped head feathers of goldfinch.
The cats rub against the screened door
with mouths full of bird, muffled meowing.
I let my cats kill for me. They think
I'm the indoor cat, lap cat, declawed. They mistake
the time I spend mesmerized by bird feeder goings-on,
for longing. I know my cats kill birds for me
because last winter I found a finch on bluish snow, dead
of natural causes, wings outstretched—
an image someone might tattoo
across a shoulder blade. I watched
from the window but didn't make a move
to move her stiff body. It was probably
my window that killed her. The cats saw me see her,
they knew I could have had her, took
them three days to disappear her: no feathers for me.

RED MEAT CURE

He went away
I couldn't eat
couldn't feed myself
lay down devastated
couldn't eat lettuce
walked hunched over
couldn't eat bread
I took meat
fat, skin, flesh
I drove miles
drove without thought
Shaker hymns played
it was spring
in the background
time of resurrection
I ate ham
I prayed hard
rivers breached banks
fields of ice
fields of ravens
I ate eggs
he stayed away
I sucked marrow
I mothered alone
the boys played
Legos were played
cars were played
magic was attempted
I slept through
I ate linguica
I ate liver
on came Valentines'
we made valentines
I cut hearts
cried while gluing
eyes on hearts
swept up scraps

down in prayer
on the floor
angle of supplication
I sought God
couldn't find God
pleaded *O God*
I mothered myself
I sweethearted myself
red meat cure
I fed myself
like a wolf
like a raven
I ate sheep
I ate venison
I ate goat
something inside me
rose up red-
toothed, two-fisted

CRONING

after Marlen Haushofer

This happens at an abandoned hunting lodge,
something like a cottage in the woods, stripped of sweet
curtains. I'm stone deaf and alone, or I'm the last person on earth.
I cut my hair with scissors meant for ordinary paper
and keep a diary peopled with starlings, grass, crickets,
thunder storms, but oddly silent. I find a gun
and learn to hunt. I obsessively paint birds, ball up the results.
I'm trying to paint a bird that, in the subtle tilt
of its head, is preparing to respond to the call of its kind.
The call doesn't come. My birds, even flocking, are alone.
If I find a dog, a cow and a cat, I'll make a menagerie
and retain my ability to nurture, keep myself familiar
for their sake. Otherwise, I'll turn my back on the room,
watch the silent landscape outside my window. Winter
is calming to my predicament with its slow and muffled
movements, transformations half-frozen. Spring
makes me anxious; mute upheaval looks like catastrophe.
There's an invisible wall that starts somewhere inside me
and extends out, hundreds of miles along the ridgeline. It does
what walls are supposed to do; it came up or came down,
ironically, because I was absent of walls,
didn't know how to construct a boundary to save my life.
Now my cracked and feral voice, too loud, like a fox holing its prey,
or calling a mate, has done what I couldn't do. One day a man appears
in my field, the one I hunt and rest in, he's standing amongst the loosestrife.
He has an axe and kills my animals for no reason.
He'd split my skull too, but I've become a good shot.

MY STUDY

I have a room of my own and call it a study.
A girl my son invites over asks,
chirpy and eager to please: *what are you studying?*
asks what are those woody-stemmed flowers
I'm arranging in a vase,
heavy-perfumed purple clusters? It's May.
She just moved up from Florida,
doesn't know the names of our birds either.
My son points out that he doesn't know the names
for most of the flowers in my garden and he's *from here*.
The two of them talk about Cuban jazz,
which my son also knows nothing about,
but his interest in this sweet girl extends
to her mother's ancestry, her father's taste in music.
This girl, who really is sweet and eager
to please, who herself studies
Mandarin and animal husbandry,
has a no-nonsense way about her,
a confident stride, asking me what I *study*.
And I can't say *everything*, can I? Can't launch
into my new interest in Ogham, the design
of Vita Sackville West's gardens,
my odd project taking daily photos
of the town's events chalkboard
as potluck supper after potluck supper is erased
and replaced, or blurred by rain.
How I don't so much *study* in my study as struggle
to hold too many things, make rope
by braiding green bark strips, then use it
to drag a pebble, like a two-ton piece of shale, an inch.
How I sometimes imagine others struggling with me.
She's not the type of girl to roll eyes and mumble
intense or *deep* under her breath, out of ear shot,
or even in her own secret thoughts.
I don't think she would.
That's why I like her. I might tell her,
as I would tell a daughter if I had one,

about the woman who got clipped on the cheek
by the fine edge of an eagle's wing as the eagle dove
for a fish beside the boat she sat in. A neat slice,
not much more than a paper cut,
but she would have been killed if the eagle
were a hair's breadth closer. A wing cut
is a kind of baptism. Which would lead me
to driving on the Williamsburg Road at dusk
the other night. I was in a Subaru, affording
no blood-sacrifice. Speeding toward me
a red-tailed hawk, level with my window.
Muscular ghost of kohl-lined eyes,
markings like ruddy tornadoes
touching down. The simultaneity was not effortless
for me: bluing dusk, a few sharp stars, my fantasy
of the hawk entering through my open window
with cutting wings—

Do you sew?
Imagine holding a row of stick-pins
between your pursed lips. Now swallow.

CRUSH THE BEEHIVES

Let's cry all night into a bowl,
blue beige the color of eggshell
but someone will interrupt,
someone will enter the room
clinking six dirty glasses,
line them up beside the sink
and turn to me, wanting
to fill the curio cabinet in my chest
with Hallmark figurines.
The bowl should be shallow
enough to measure cryfall.
or someone will sit down heavily
at my feet with a sigh that says
its fixable by me
and my doors will fly open
against my will. Someone will
wander in, crush the beehives
and the nests, toss my broken
glass collection, rearrange
the plants by time of death.
But I don't want to cry all night,
and I don't want to waste time
wresting back my summer dusk, so quickly thinning
from honey to dust . . .
fill the eggshell bowl with my personal ocean,
already filled with someone else's
keys, lighter, change.
If *I* wash it, *I* want it
left alone on the kitchen counter—
space unto itself,
un of other people's *stuff.*
The kitchen is dealt
a last down-thrust of sunlight
through the window, shaft
through my eye. I sit at the table, crying
all over my bare arms like a twenty-year-old—she
over an emptiness to fill. I
can't convince her the emptiness is good.

WEBCAM: PEMAQUID POINT LIGHTHOUSE

the image will automatically refresh every five minutes

At 5 am the frame may be black,
but the ocean's right there
if I could hear it, beating
against striations of iconic rock.
I'm not sure when the light goes dark,
it's on a timer like the webcam
and their syncopation's off.
On other days at 5 am the light,
as they say, is a beacon;
casts its bluish haze over the ground,
as they say, *sweeping*,
but which looks to me like an ultrasound,
the light in its center a fetus.

With each *refresh* day advances.
I usually miss that moment *dawn*
because it happens in the interval
and I suspect the webcam's
five minutes is closer to ten.
The sky is dark, the sky is light.
There's the rough outcrop, whitewashed
lighthouse anchored in rock but tipped
toward the silver, viscous ocean.
In one frame the scene is nature's,
then there's a girl
mid-sprint on the yellow grass,
running away from me.

WYETH PAINTS HER ROOM

There's not much *her* in the room: the hand
that pinned the filmy curtains back

as a woman pulls her hair up off her neck,
conch on the table, shells lined up on a sill,

the largest a matchbox boat's sail,
the smallest a child's thumbnail.

But what she hasn't arranged is still attributable
somehow to her: the way he brushes sun

across the open door, sharper
sunlight like a letter opener on the table,

her view through feathered glass. The artist paints
a vertical, body's-width of entryway

like himself eavesdropping at her threshold,
a latent unease like the foundation

coat of beige beneath layers of beige.
When does distance become absence? Are they

hues of the same longing? Windows fill with gray
sea, the white sky tempera-luminous. As he works

the wind picks up, takes the door like a sail
and slams it wide, rattling the light in its transit.

He stands in the center of the cold space,
in the corner, beside the window,

to really *see* it without her. The fraying curtain
like the hem of a nightgown. Emerson said, *Without*

electricity the air would rot. Cady Stanton said, *more profound*
than the midnight sea; the solitude of self.

While he painted, his wife Betsy stood
on the opposite side of their island.

NOT THE SAME BIRD TWICE

When I called for him outside, birds
mimicked his meow; not cat birds,
not even the same bird twice.
Near the drainage pipe,
when I thought I heard a sound like air
escaping from a tire, or in the woods, a far-off
plaintive call for help. But coyote and great-
horned owl don't kidnap cats for later.
Around here, by the time you realize
the cat's gone missing
it's probably in the last stages
of another animal's digestion.

When I called for him in the crawl space
I felt a century of domesticated ghosts
undrowse and rouse themselves, some
plastic sheeting rustled,
a long yawning silence stretched.
And above, the spring day heated up.
A cow licked the entire head of its calf. The neighbor
on chemo clutched her side—white as a thin
scrim of snow on the greening hill,
white as bleached bone with the grass
grown through, wild phlox; wild
as the soft purring of birds.

HOME MOVIES

My baby's mouth is open in the video,
my one-month-old baby just introduced
to the camera. His name, said for the first time
for an audience of my wider family in other states.
His name said like a novelty, still strange to the tongue,
and his birthdate and birth weight announced.
Someone is talking to him
and the camera focuses on his face
as he kicks and fidgets on the changing table.
Someone is saying, as someone always says
in these home movies, *say hi to grammy,*
say hi to auntie, say hi, say hi.
And every time, he opens his mouth so wide
it's a black hole matching his wide black eyes
(I can almost smell his milky breath).
A high-pitched squeal like *hi* comes out,
so someone keeps saying *say hi,* back and
forth it goes. My baby knows he's
doing something right, getting the treat of
soft voices and smiles. *He's a genius,* my voice
in the background still thick with pregnancy hormones,
half sarcastic with the sarcasm that came down
through my father's side. And then the camera is on me
and yes my face is still swollen from pregnancy,
my father beside me, the only person in the family
completely unfazed by the enormous camcorder.
Then it's a birthday party, someone is telling my
four-year-old to say hi to grammy, say hi to my grandmother
whose been gone a decade now, *for Lil* written
on the side of the chunky black video. *None of us*
share one cell with our former selves, my eighteen-year-old
informs me as we watch. Someone's saying *ask your mommy.*
Then my four-year-old yelling *mommy*
as he leaves in search of me. But the camera
stays put, scanning the room in a house we don't own anymore,
the floor littered with wrapping paper, balloons risen to the ceiling.
As the camera rests on them, people wave,

say an overdone, or awkward *hi*, then resume conversation.
And the camera moves on. It finds me washing my baby
in the kitchen sink. Or this could be another day. I can't tell.
I'm saying, *he's just like his brother* . . .
then, *I shouldn't compare them, I do that too much.*
I'm telling my four-year-old he can't
go outside alone. His husky voice pleads *mommy?*
My tired voice says *no.* I want to tell my younger self
she shouldn't feel guilty, because she'll end up feeling
guilty every day about what she can't or won't give.
The restless camera turns from me as I apologize
to my four-year-old with a popsicle.
Back in the living room, the sun has slid
down the wall, but people are still deep in conversation;
boring to watch at a remove of fifteen years with bad audio.
They talk on. Demanding, it seems,
we observe their lives, their obsolescence.

FLINCH

Midsummer Sunday, hot,
and I'm driving the back roads
I take when I'm not in a hurry.
Even the shade is warm, moss
and lichen lit. And I don't pass
another driver until that pick-up
truck rattles toward me
at the curve in the road that means
I'm almost in town. I wonder
if the dam is open, the water
rushing into free fall, frothing a boil.
I wonder if the white dove is flying
its swooping circuit, under the steel
rafters of the bridge,
over the flowers with a flock
of dun and gray doves. Or if
the pair of eagles is nesting further up river
and I might spend 15 minutes watching them
fish their dinner before it's time
to get what I came for:
milk and oil and eggs. At the curve
in the road there's a frost heave still
to be smoothed out, where the pick-up
bounces a couple times on rusty shocks,
truckbed rattling and crunching, truckbed coughing
up an old lawnmower. Over the side
it rolls with ease, flies horizontally
toward my windshield, driver's side. Flinch.
I'm already squared for impact, hands tight,
fingers wide on the wheel,
instinctual swerve as if I could escape
a flying lawnmower
inches from my stunned face-under-glass.
A lawnmower, influenced maybe, by a change
in the wind; my grandmother, seven years
dead; my other grandmother, gone ten; the simple fact
that I want badly enough to see eagles today.

A lawnmower that stops threatening me,
like a dog someone called off,
rights itself, sticks a perfect landing
in the street. I think it even rolls
nonchalantly away, looking more like a lawnmower
looking for a patch of grass than a freak accident.
But I don't know because I keep driving,
not thinking
about clods of someone else's lawn dislodged,
green and still fragrant all over my broken . . .
I wouldn't laugh, but how could anyone not
think *humiliating*
coming across an obituary with a lawnmower in it
and nowhere a mention of blades.

ALONE IN MY OWN WOODS

I know I live half alive in the world,
I know half my life belongs to the wild darkness.

—GALWAY KINNELL

The setting sun through leaves
tinks like a spoon tink tinking,
tink . . . tink . . . tink on thin trunks,
the birches' sad eyes. And I find myself wanting the sun to stop
its restless fidgeting. The family just driven off,
I have a vague goal: how much silence can I imbibe
in two hours, how completely can I forget myself?
The soil is so black I consider going back
out into the light for the yellow wheelbarrow
with the rock-sized hole in the bottom, shoving it over
the crumbled stone wall, fighting it uphill to this spot
where the air is fragrant with leaf rot.
I do my best work on a whim, barefooted.
But I'm project-weary, distracted by the time-lapsed
image of myself over many years, building up to ret down
the perfect compost pile while decades of leaf-fall gently decay,
without the aid of accelerating pellets,
just beyond the treeline. There are glacial deposits
all through these woods, chunks of quartz,
bleach-white and sparkling, here and here,
like something more alien to this place than I am.
I used to sit on a quartz boulder in the woods
up behind the house, its table-top-flatness moist and cold,
and pray hard for certain circumstances
I couldn't live without. Beside the boulder
a cave made by an uprooted tree I imagined
sheltered a bear or coyote that might, when I was most quiet,
most vulnerable, growl low from that still dark place
just inside the hole. And I would see its eyes glow dim.
And it would see me.
That night I would not have returned home.

NOTES

"Don't you forget about me": quotes lyrics from the Simple Minds song of the same title.

"See the Wolf": In the common slang of late 1600s France, when Charles Perrault penned his version of "Little Red Riding Hood," a girl who lost her innocence or virginity was said to have "seen the wolf."

"Codeine Metempsychosis": Metempsychosis is defined, in part, as the transmigration of the soul from a human or animal to some other human or animal body.

"Real Fairy Tale" was informed by Jean Cocteau's 1946 adaptation of "Beauty and the Beast," as well as by *Postmodern Fairy Tales: Gender and Narrative Strategies* by Cristina Bacchilega and *The Bloody Chamber and Other Stories* by Angela Carter.

"Croning" is after two novels by Marlen Haushofer: *The Wall* and *The Loft*.

"More Than the Weight of Its Laden Branches": The italicized passages are from a *New Yorker* article written by Rachel Aviv titled "God Knows Where I Am" about schizophrenia and the tragedy of Linda Bishop.

ACKNOWLEDGMENTS

Barn Owl Review: "See the Wolf"

BlazeVOX: *"Don't you forget about me"*

CavanKerry Online: "More Than the Weight of Its Laden Branches"

Fourteen Hills: "You Are Not Grass"

Fugue: "Sisters, 1980s"

Gallery of Readers Anthology: "Alone in My Own Woods"

Southern Poetry Review: "Self Portrait with Mabel, Rose, Lillianne, Fern, Mildred, Bea"

Spoon River Poetry Review: "Wyeth Paints *Her Room*"

Tuesday; An Art Project: "Crush the Beehives"

I would like to thank CavanKerry Press and Joan Cusack Handler for publishing *See the Wolf* in the Emerging Voices series alongside so many stellar poets, Starr Troup for making the pre-publication process not just seamless but enjoyable, and Baron Wormser for his generous reading of, and guidance with, the manuscript. I would also like to thank Karyna McGlynn, Jennifer Sweeney and Meredith Sibley. I am always thankful to my family: Ray, Sebastian and Tobias for being my best friends, first readers, talented artists who inspire me to work harder and, most of all, my greatest loves. Finally, thank you to my mom for single-parenting both a rebellious daughter and an overly-sensitive daughter through some rough terrain with love and understanding.

CAVANKERRY'S MISSION

CavanKerry Press is committed to expanding the reach of poetry to a general readership by publishing poets whose works explore the emotional and psychological landscapes of everyday life.

OTHER BOOKS IN THE EMERGING VOICES SERIES